Muck
and the Machine Convoy

Sumsy
and the Sunflower Spill

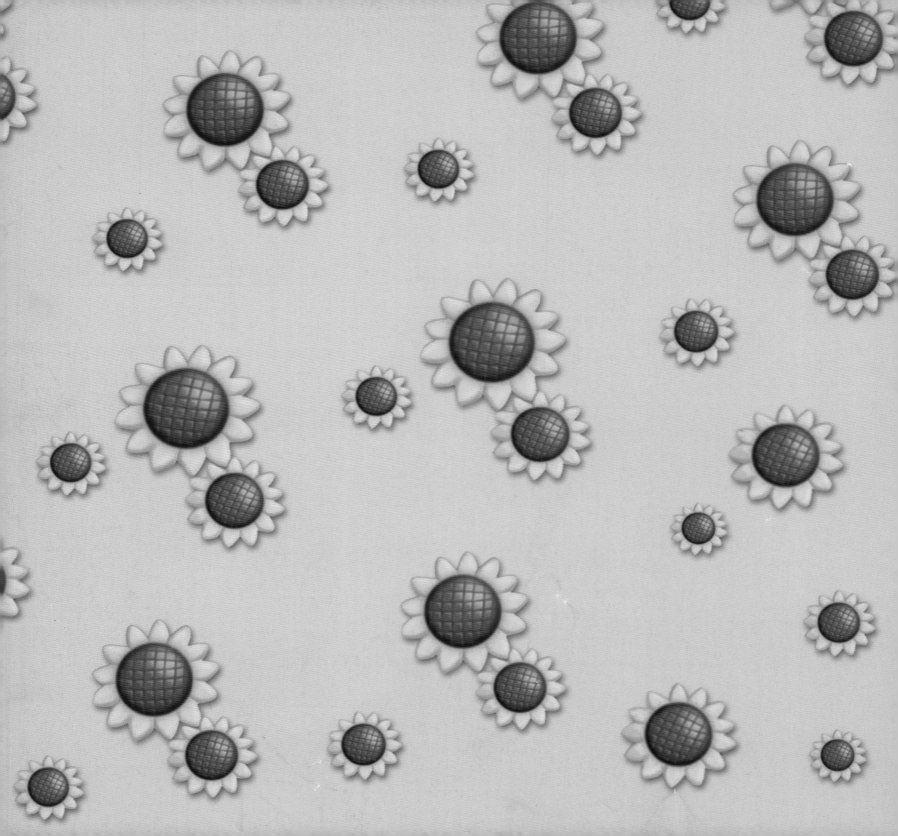

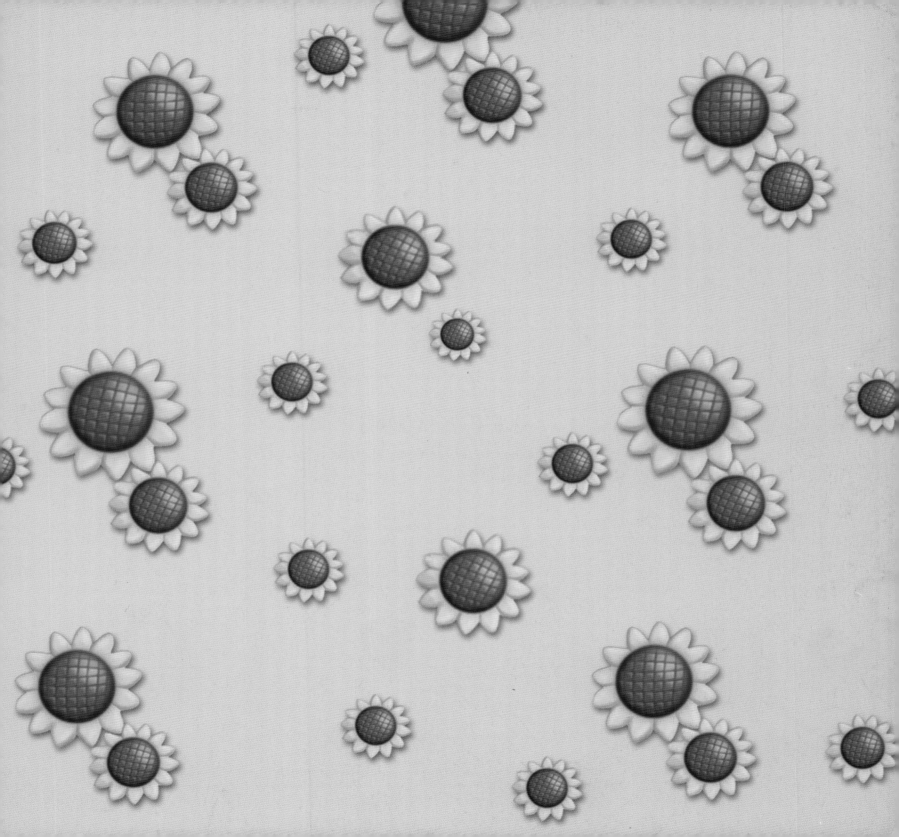

EGMONT

We bring stories to life

This edition published for BCA in 2008
First published in Great Britain 2008
by Egmont UK Limited,
239 Kensington High Street, London W8 6SA

HiT entertainment

ISBN 978 0 6035 6381 2

1 3 5 7 9 10 8 6 4 2
Printed in Italy

CONTENTS

Muck
and the Machine Convoy

Sumsy
and the Sunflower Spill

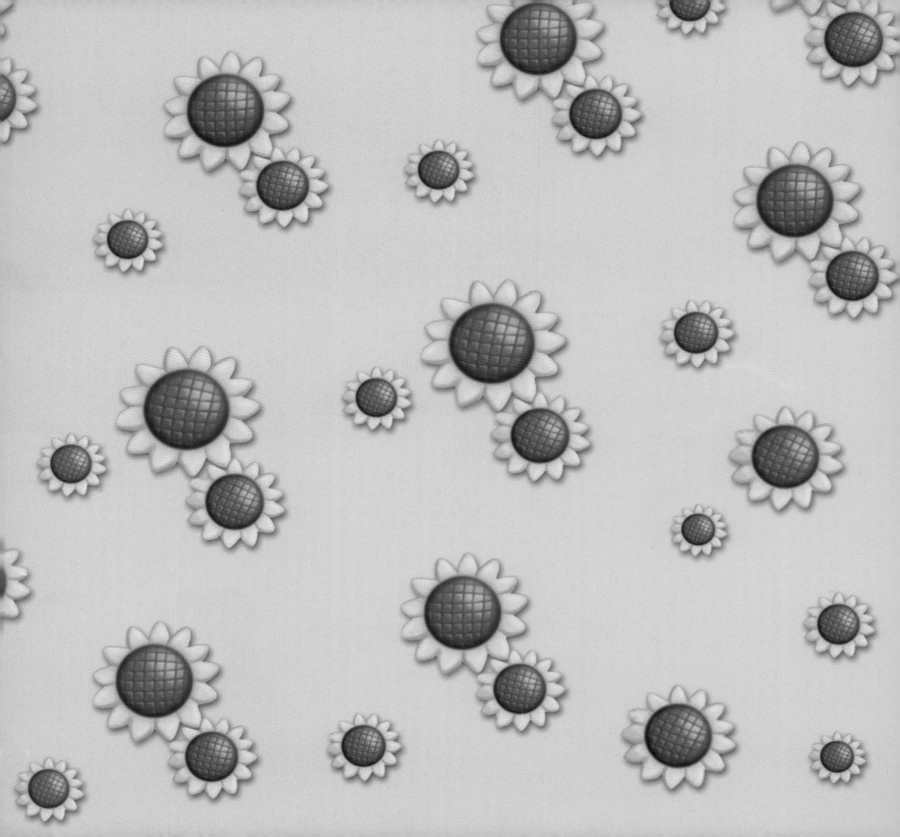

Muck
and the Machine Convoy

Illustrations by Jerry Smith

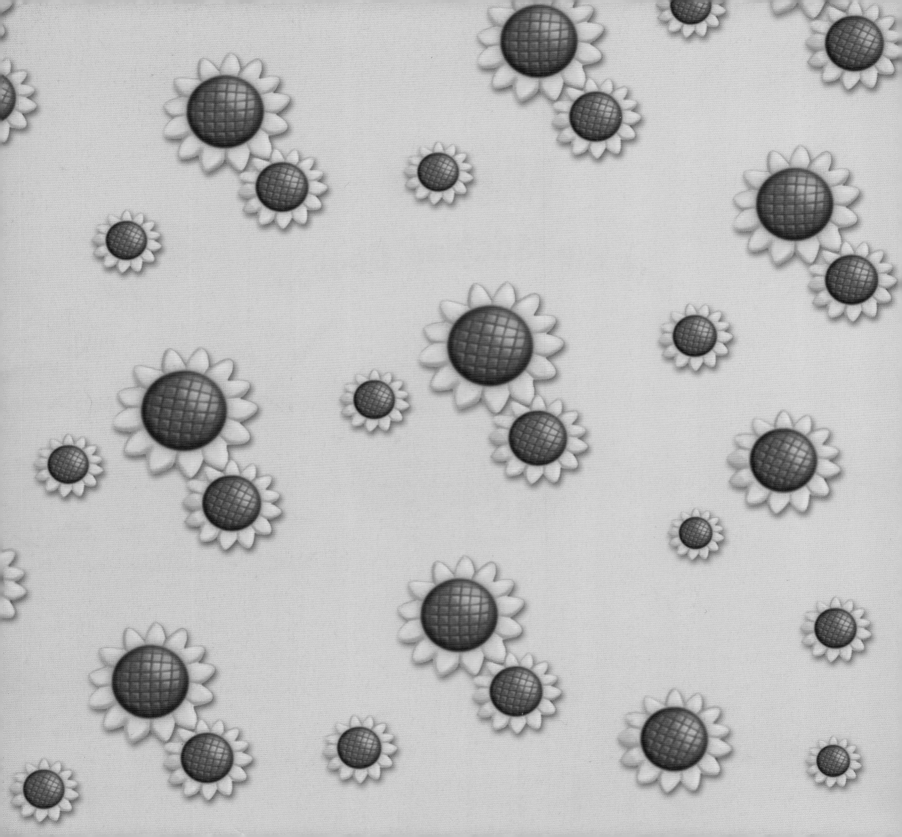

The Old Watermill needs
a new waterwheel. Muck
is given the job of leader,
but can he lead the
machines safely to the mill?

Bob and the team were going to build
a waterwheel for the Old Watermill.

"How will it work?" wondered Scoop.

Bob explained that the flow of the river
fills the buckets, which push the waterwheel
round. The wheel turns the cogs inside the mill.
Then, the cogs turn big stones that rub
together and crush the grain into flour.

"Water power! Cool!" said Muck.

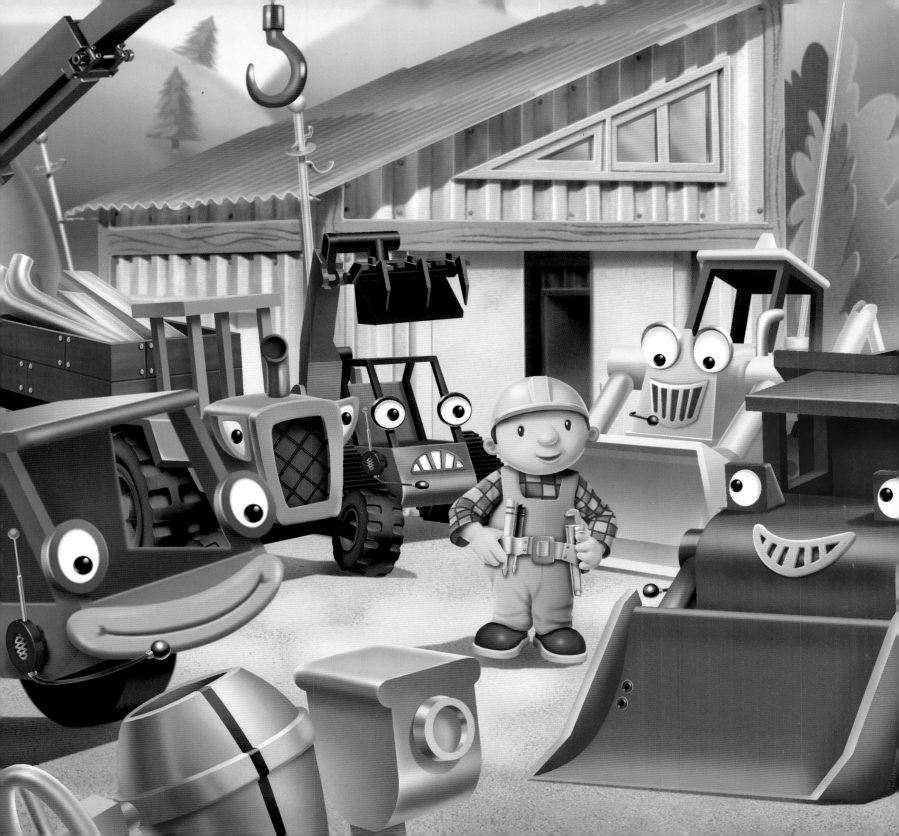

"We have to take the waterwheel to the mill," said Bob. "It comes apart, so we can take it in pieces."

Bob climbed up the ladder and loosened some nuts and screws. Lofty carefully put the pieces in Muck's tipper and Scoop's scoop, and the final part on to Benny's forklift.

The parts were heavy. It was going to be a bumpy ride!

"Muck, you will be in charge of the convoy," said Bob.

"Erm . . . Bob, what's a convoy?" he asked.

"It's when a group of machines follow each other in a line," Bob said. "You will be the leader because you can flatten a path with your caterpillar tracks for the others to follow."

Muck's new job made him feel special. He didn't want to make any mistakes.

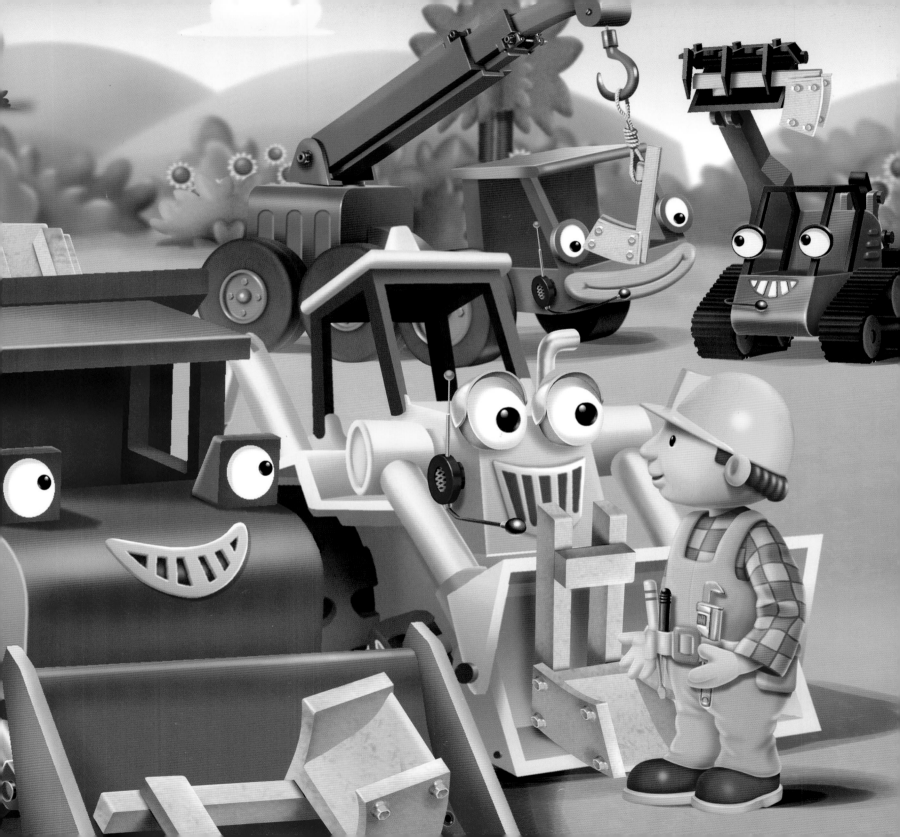

Bob told Muck how to get to the Old Watermill. "But remember," he said, "don't go into the marshland, or you'll get stuck."

"Can Muck lead us?" said Scoop.

"Yes, he can," called the team.

"Er, yeah. I hope so," worried Lofty.

"You can rely on Muck! Convoy – follow me!" said Muck, whizzing ahead. Benny, Scoop and Lofty rolled along behind him.

Bob, Travis and Dizzy took a short cut to take the scaffolding to the mill, where Wendy was waiting. The convoy was doing well.

On the way they saw a line of ducks waddle across the track. "Oh, hello, duckies. You're in a convoy just like us!" chuckled Muck.

But there was no time to stop and talk, so Muck and the team hurried on.

Meanwhile, at the Old Watermill, Bob and Wendy had almost finished the scaffolding.

"I wonder what's taking Muck so long?" thought Bob. "I'll call him on the talkie-talkie," he said. "Bob to Muck. How are you doing? Over."

"Umm . . . hello, Bob. We're doing . . . really well," said Muck, quietly.

"Great. See you soon. Over," said Bob.

But Muck and the convoy weren't doing well, at all. "Are you sure you went the right way, Muck?" asked Lofty.

"Quiet, please. Your leader needs to think!" huffed Muck, and rolled along bravely. But he was soon feeling glum.

"Oh, no! We're right back where we started!" moaned Benny.

The convoy was back at the yard!

By now, Muck and the convoy were feeling very tired.

Finally, they reached the river. "Well done, Muck! We're nearly there!" cheered Lofty.

"I did it! Let's cut across the marsh. It'll be quicker," said Muck, rolling down the riverbank.

But the convoy didn't follow at once. "I'm sure Muck knows what he's doing," urged Scoop. "Follow the leader!"

Schlup . . . schlup . . . schlup went their wheels through the muddy marsh.

Poor Lofty, his wheels had sunk deep into the mud. "You said you wouldn't get me stuck, Muck!" he bawled.

"This is all my fault. Leaders shouldn't make mistakes," worried Muck.

The ducklings were crossing the marsh, too. But one was stuck, like Lofty. The mother duck gave it a push, and the duckling waddled free.

Watching the ducks gave Lofty an idea.

He pushed Lofty with all his might. Slowly, Lofty eased out of the marsh and on to the track.

"Someone else should be leader. I've made too many mistakes," sighed Muck.

"Bob always says good leaders are ones who make a mistake and then put it right. And you did just that!" said Scoop, kindly.

The team got back in line, ready for Muck to lead them to the Watermill.

Finally, Muck's convoy arrived at the mill. "I'm sorry, Bob," mumbled Muck. "We went in a big circle . . . and got lost. Then Lofty got stuck in the marsh . . ."

"Muck did a brilliant job leading us here," said Scoop.

"Yeah, he was like unreal banana peel!" joined in Benny.

"Well done, Muck," cheered Bob. Muck beamed happily with everyone's praise.

"Now, let's finish building the waterwheel," said Bob. With all the team helping, it was soon complete. Bob turned the handle outside, and slowly, the waterwheel began to turn.

"Hooray!" cheered the team.

Just then, the mother duck and her ducklings floated past on the river.

"Looks like we both got our convoys here safely!" Muck said, proudly.

THE END

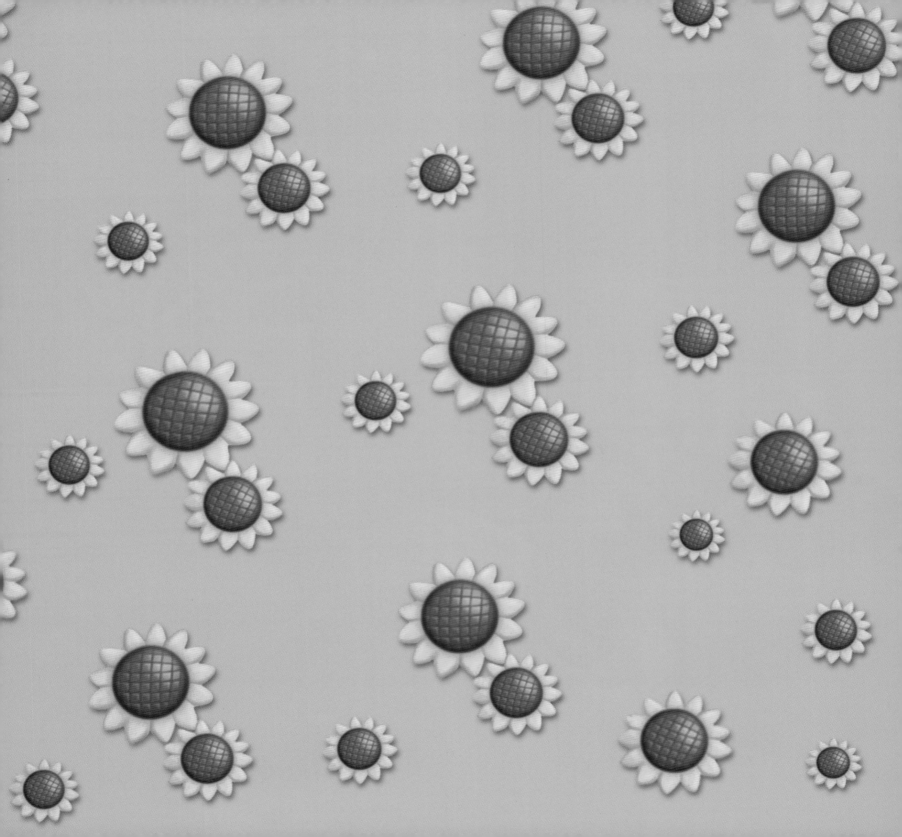

Sumsy
and the Sunflower Spill

Illustrations by Craig Cameron

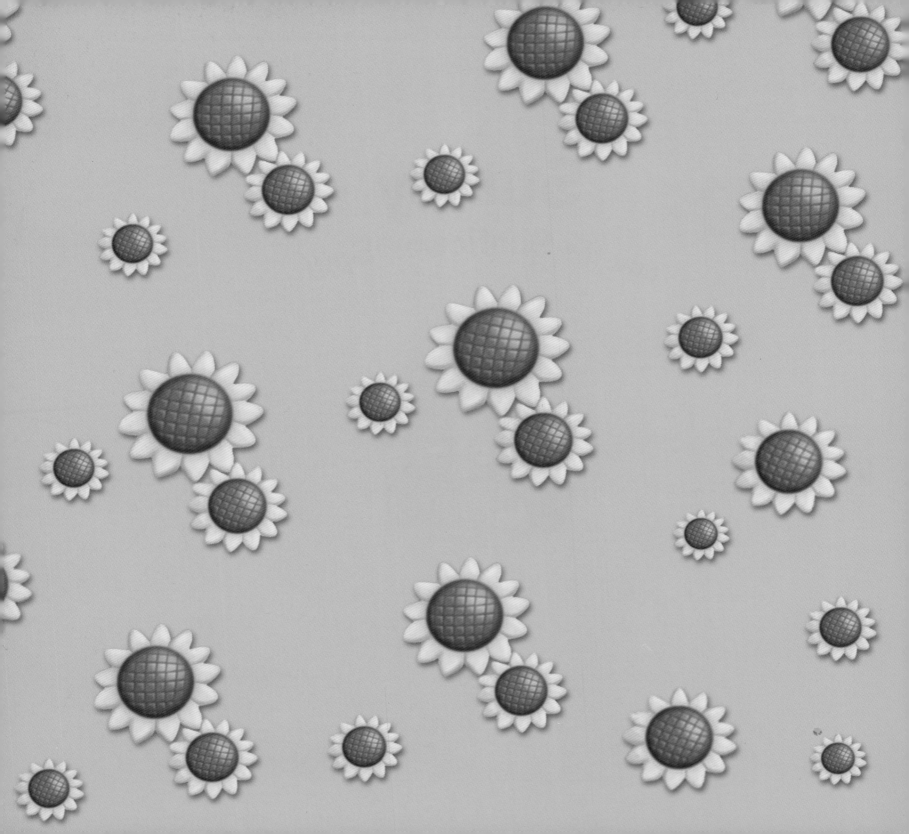

Farmer Pickles' Sunflower Oil
Factory is almost ready to open!
There's just one more job to do.
Sumsy arrives to help, but will
the factory open on time?

Farmer Pickles was getting ready for the grand opening of his new Sunflower Oil Factory.

"There's just one more job to do," he said. "I need somewhere for all these boxes."

"No problem," smiled Bob. "We'll build you a bottle depot."

"Thanks, Bob," said Farmer Pickles. "Now I've got a surprise for you! Meet . . ."

"Sumsy the forklift! She's going to move the boxes with the bottles of sunflower oil from the factory to the storage depot."

"I can pack 'em! I can stack 'em!" smiled Sumsy. "Hi, everyone!"

"Hello, Sumsy," said Bob, Scoop and Travis.

She looked at Travis. "One, two, three boxes. I love counting!" Sumsy laughed."

"Right!" said Bob. "I'd better get started building this depot." And off he went.

Farmer Pickles and Travis went too, and Scoop and Sumsy were left on their own.

"I'm Scoop!" said Scoop. "I know everything about Sunflower Valley. I'll show you around. Follow me!"

"What about the boxes?" Sumsy worried. But Scoop had rolled away.

The first stop on Scoop's tour was the homestead. Then he showed Sumsy the workshops and the storerooms. "We've plenty of time to work," said Scoop.

But Sumsy looked sad. She knew there were lots of boxes to be moved.

Soon, they reached the site where Bob and the team were building the bottle depot.

"Hi, Scoop!" smiled Dizzy.

"Hi, everyone," called Scoop. "This is Sumsy!
Sumsy, meet Dizzy, Muck and . . . Roley."

"Rock and ro-ho-ole!" said Roley.

"Three machines. Three!" counted Sumsy.
"Three boxes is how many I can fit on my forklift.
I can pack 'em, I can stack 'em!" she laughed, and
raced away.

Just then, Farmer Pickles arrived with a big crate. "Look what I've got here!" he said. "A bottle-labelling machine."

He pressed a button and labels began to fly out, sticking themselves to Dizzy, Roley and Bob!

"We're not bottles! Ha, ha!" smiled Dizzy.

"What a sticky situation!" said Farmer Pickles. "I hope Sumsy brings those boxes of bottles soon."

Inside the factory, Sumsy was hard at work. "Coming through! Ten bottles in every box," she said, whizzing past Scoop.

"Wait!" moaned Scoop. I haven't shown you all the factory yet! How can I tell you things if you keep driving off?"

Sumsy raced away, with Scoop chasing behind.

Scoop caught up with Sumsy and swerved in front of her to make her stop.

Sumsy screeched to a halt, but it was too late. CRASH! The boxes flew off her forklift and smashed on the ground.

"Oh, no!" cried Scoop.

Sumsy and Scoop went to look at the mess. The bottles were broken and oil had spilled everywhere.

Meanwhile, Bob and the team had nearly finished building the bottle depot.

"Well done, team. We're almost ready for your bottles, Farmer Pickles," he said.

"But then we need labels on the bottles," worried Farmer Pickles. "Where's Sumsy?"

"Here she comes!" said Dizzy, as Sumsy trundled sadly towards them.

Farmer Pickles saw the boxes of broken bottles. "Oh dear!" he gasped.

"I'm sorry, Farmer Pickles," said Sumsy. "I was trying to do my job, when, erm . . ."

"It was me," said Scoop. "I got in Sumsy's way. I was showing her around the valley."

When Scoop found out that the bottles all needed labels, he felt very sorry. "There's not enough time!" he cried.

"Three boxes fit on my forklift, and two fit in your digger," Sumsy said to Scoop, kindly. "We'll work together to get the job done quicker!"

So that's what they did. Before long, all the boxes were safely in the depot and all the bottles had labels.

Bob finished building the depot wall and the factory was ready to open, just in time!

The grand opening was the next day.
"I declare this Sunflower Oil Factory open!" said
Farmer Pickles. And he snipped the ribbon in half.

"Hooray for Farmer Pickles!" cheered Bob.

"And hooray for Sumsy and Scoop!" said Farmer
Pickles, proudly.

"Ha, ha!" laughed Sumsy. "When we work together,
it's as easy as one, two, three!"

THE END

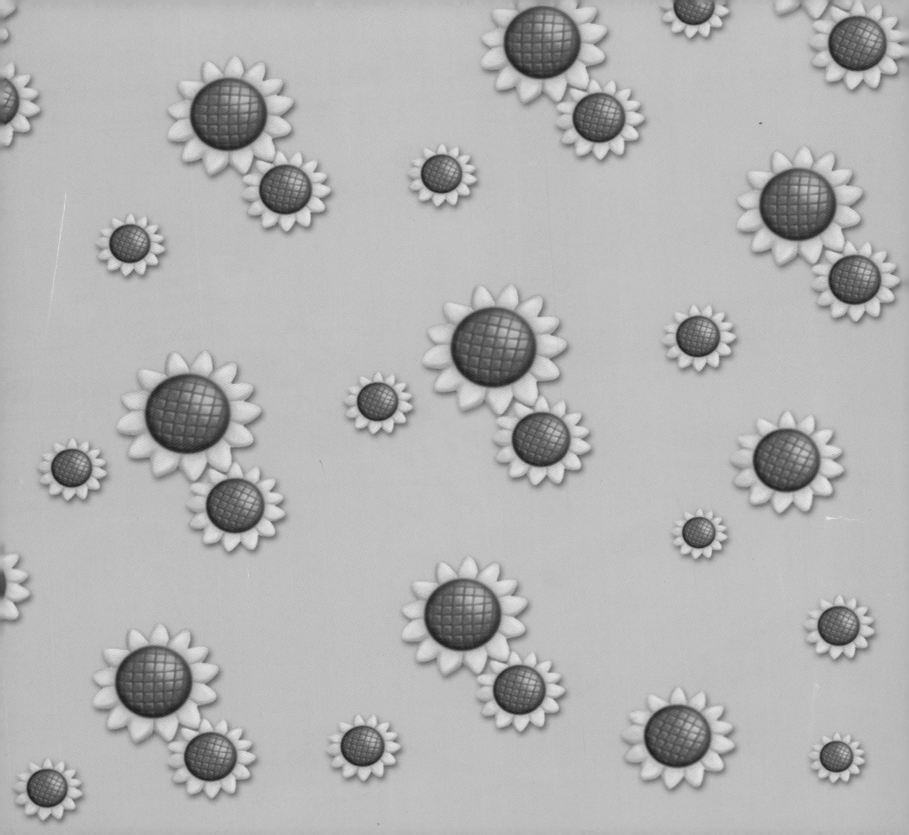

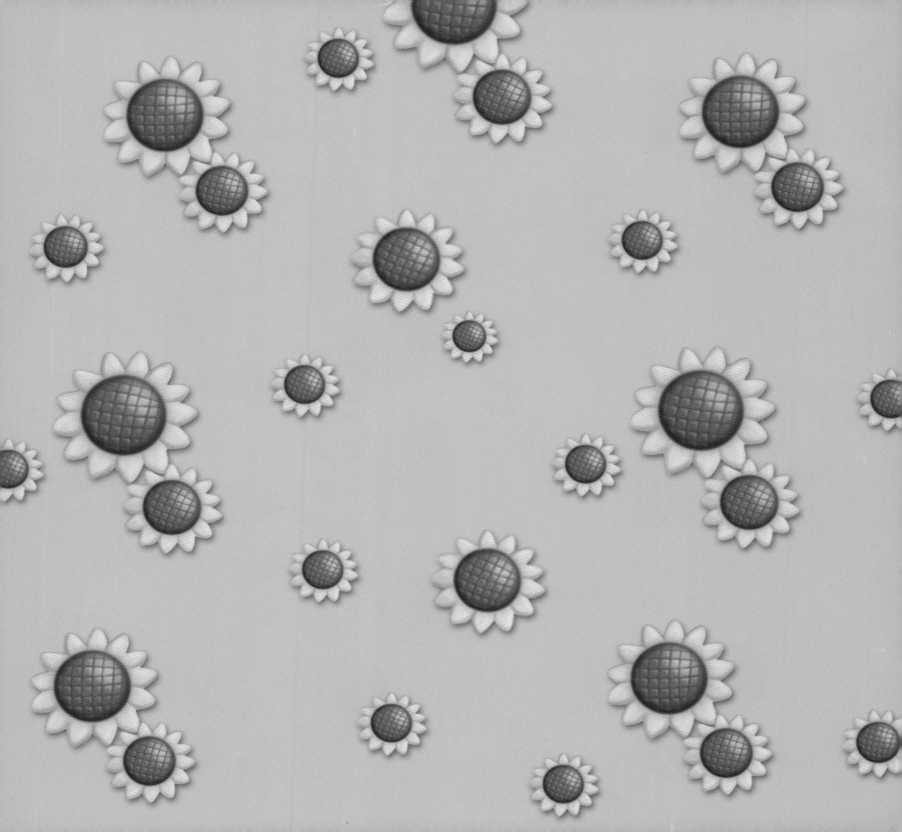

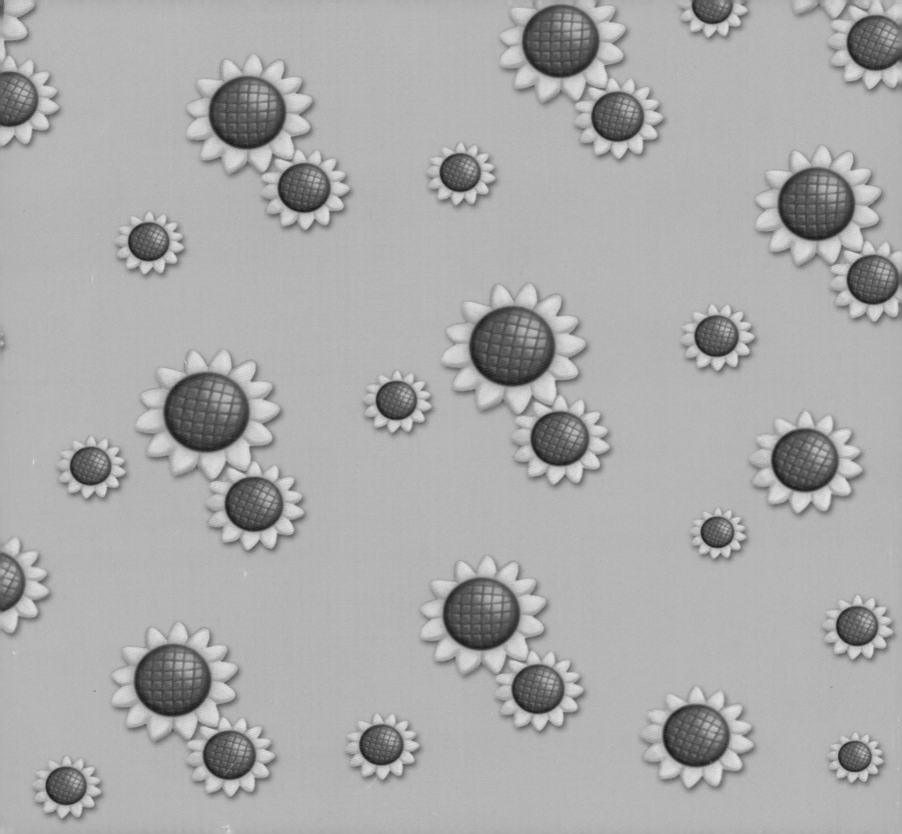